Sanitarium

BOBBY BOYD

Contents

Ch. 1
"Not Hearing Me"

Dr. Beth Dickson and her patients had a little one on one on why she felt the way she feels and does the things that she does. They sat and talked for about twenty minutes before Amanda went into her ways of expressing herself in the only way she knows how.

Amanda: He came back night after night and touched me like no other. He opened me like a jar of jelly. Hearing the pop sound fresh and it felt good. He ran his hands down my body and it sent chills all over me front to back like a cool breeze gliding by your face. Made me feel some type of way inside and out.

Dr. Beth: How did you know at this time that it was bad?

Amanda smiles looking into Dr. Beth's eyes with a glassy look in her eyes.

Amanda: I can feel what you're thinking. I know that you think I'm talking about that son of a bitch guardian of mine. Because you don't believe in someone being in a room with you when others see just you.

Dr. Beth: Ok, let's talk about your guardian.

Amanda: Come on, Dr., you know all about that fucker. You know I cut his balls off. I cut his dick in half like a banana straight down the middle so I could hear him scream at the top of his lungs. I sat next to him and watched him bleed out like a gutted pig until he died...painful. It was the only way for him to stop.

Dr. Beth: Stop what?

Amanda: Stop fucking me!! You're not listening, Dr.

Dr. Beth: I am, Amanda.

Amanda: You're not listening with your heart, just your brain, and it is a problem. You, Dr.

Beth, are on the outside looking in and you have no idea how it feels to not be trusted.

Dr. Beth: Look at me, Amanda, you have to trust me, too.

Amanda: How can I trust someone who thinks I'm crazy? Add that to your notes, Dr.

Dr. Beth: Fair enough... We will pick back up tomorrow. I think we made a breakthrough.

Amanda got up then Dr. Beth stood up. They looked at each other in the eye. No smile, no emotion, just a blank stare toward one another as Amanda grabbed Dr. Beth by her wrist and squeezed it a little.

Amanda: Tell me, doc, do you know what it is to feel like this inside out? Tell me, "You will get yours".

Dr. Beth: Amanda, you're hurting me.

A woman's voice spoke on the outside of the halls. "Let the doctor go, Amanda". The woman behind the desk hollard for the guard to come and pull Amanda's grip off the Dr. They go back

*and forth for about six seconds and Amanda
then let's go.*

*Amanda: I did…I'm not holding the good doc!!!
You can see I'm not holding her, let me go!
The guard came in and grabbed Amanda from
behind and was pulling her away so she could calm
down as she kicks, hollers, and fights. Looking at
Dr. Beth as she gets taken away, she said, "I'm not
touching her!!!" Dr. Beth just looked and grabbed
her papers off the table from where she and
Amanda were sitting face to face. Then she took a
deep breath and started to walk out. The guard
took Amanda and went left as the Doctor went to
the right. She went through the sliding doors and
didn't seem too happy. As she was walking, she
could still hear Amanda fighting and hollering.*

Amanda: Let me go, you're making me mad.

Guard: Please, Amanda, stop it!

Amanda: Fuck off me.

*Then the other guard opens the main gate to the
main hall—a long hallway where the girls are
locked up for hours and hours at a time with
only a small window to look out of. Dr. Beth*

started walking down that long hallway knowing that Amanda is not too far behind; to hear any more remarks from her till they put her back in her room locked down. Amanda is still fighting for the guard to let her go as she sees Dr. Beth.

Amanda:
Let me go… okay, okay I can walk by myself.

The doctor was a few feet in front of the guard and the nurse plus Amanda. As she walked down the hallway passing Amanda's room, she heard Amanda mocking and acting out behind her. Dr. Beth never turned around to see what Amanda was doing, she just kept walking and listening.

Amanda: Awww… look at the beautiful doctor walk away in her high-profile degree and her keep-your-head-up shoulders back; you all that huh…Doc…look at me. "Hey, doc, miss little all that". You are not all that. You not better than everyone else, you hear me?

Guard: Get in your room.

Then Dr. Beth continues to walk… thinking to herself, Amanda may be nuts. She gets to the end of the hallway and goes through another door.

She passed another guard then she makes a right, headed up the stairs, passed a few more windows and doors, then she went through a sliding steel door passing two more guards.

Guard: How are you doing?

Dr. Beth: I'm fine, thank you.

Then Dr. Beth went through another gate where it says on the wall, "You are now leaving the main lock up", as she walks down another long hallway with her black dress pants, three-inch heels, black and grey four-buttons short-sleeved shirt. She makes it to the side and starts walking up a level of stairs. She goes up seven, then turns and goes up another seven till she gets to the third floor. She walks down the hallway passing two people on her right side. She comes up on a door at the end of the hallway. Dr. Beth reaches out and opens the door and see Allie Mae (one of the top doctors/chief that runs the staff head) doing paperwork at her desk.
She didn't hear Beth open her door and pop her head in. She looked up before Beth said, "Hey," and she jumped.

Allie Mae: Geez...you scared the living...WOW!

Dr. Beth: Sorry...I need to cross-reference some names and a few things. I'd like to look through a few files with you if you have the time on Tuesday?

Ellie Mae: Go by and check with Donna. She'll give you a time where we could take care of things.

Dr. Beth: Okay, thank you, and sorry for walking in.

Allie Mae: It's okay! Please shut my door back.

She headed down the hall to her husband's office, Mr. Peter Dickson. As she gets to the door, she could hear his voice on the phone, so she walks in.

Peter: No, no, I will not discharge her, not going to happen. If you want to beg the difference, have a judge order her transfer, that'll be fine with me. Till that happens, she should stay here. Thank you!

Peter hung up the phone and said to himself: "Some people", as Dr. Beth walked in the office.

Peter: Hey, how are you? What's on your mind? I can see your face.

Ch. 2
"Distorted"

Dr. Beth: Amanda...she scares her stepfather again. She says something is visiting her in her cell.

Peter: I see!

Dr. Beth: It's the third time in a month. I think it may have something to do with the way she looks at her stepfather. Hmmm, maybe remorse. But instead of assessing the thoughts and accepting it, Amanda just falls into steps of satanic meanderings. Peter: Beth, she needs time. You know in time all things heel.

Dr. Beth: I've given it time. To Vonda, Jill, and Ivey: I don't know, maybe they're too drugged up, too medicated. I know we all create our reality in life. Yes, agreed, but what Amanda creates is so, so far from any objective reality.

Peter: Amanda's mind... it runs away.

Dr. Beth: Well, right now my mind is running on tired.

Peter sat in his chair looking and listening to Dr. Beth go on and on about Amanda. Then he got up and rubbed his hands together. He walked towards the bar that he has in his office. He told her, "Please come here, get up and stand beside me".

Peter: You have a brilliant mind, you'll come up with something.

He gets two glasses out and holds them up, then tells her, "Look at this glass, it's empty". Then he gives the glass to her and tells her to hold it as he pours some water into it. He tells her to look in the glass as the water moves back and forward.

Peter: This is what she sees. Now keep looking.

Dr. Beth: A distorted image of herself.

Peter: Who are you in all of this?

Dr. Beth: I'm a reflection.

Peter: You are reflections.

Dr. Beth: If I'm the reflection, then she's the image.

Dr. Beth looks at Peter. He looks him in the eye and asks him, "Now, who are you?"

Peter: I can see both of you...always remember the skill to repress, and we'll see the survival tool without it. Amanda might not have survived.

Dr. Peter looks at Dr. Beth, walks right up to her and smiles, then he tells her she will work it out and that she's beautiful. Then they share a kiss. As Dr. James Stockson walks and saw them kissing, he weighs in on their moment with choice words of his own.

Dr. James: Oh, my apologies for interrupting the love moment between a lovely couple.

Dr. Peter: Dr. James Stockson, no need for apologies. I and Dr. Beth were going over repression as a survival mechanism.

Dr. James: Oh, I see. I tell you what, Dr. Peter, I had this dream a few nights ago, and boy I'm trying to forget that.

Dr. Peter: Well, I'm sure whatever you dreamt about was fascinating, doctor, but time is not on my side and I'm on my way out.

Dr. Peter grabs his case files and two personal small bottles of gin. Dr. James was trying to leave as Dr. Peter tells him, "No, no, I'm out".

Dr. Peter: I have a run that I need to make. I'm meeting up with someone.

He walks over to his wife, hugs her, and whispers, "Don't let him bore you with his crazy dream stories". Then he kisses Dr. Beth on the cheek and turns to walk out.

As the door passed Dr. James, his wife speaks out, "I'll be working, Dear, see you later."

So he stopped in front of Dr. James and tells him, "Take care of my wife while I'm gone."

Dr. James smiles. "Will do".

Dr. Peter: Good day you two.

Dr. James: See you later, boss.

Dr. James turns and looks at Dr. Beth. "The boss wants me to look after you."

Dr. James: How about we get a cup of coffee?

Dr. Beth: Mmmm, oh, that sounds good right now it's not even funny. But sadly, I've got work to do.

Dr. James: Oh, come on, Beth I'm buying. Okay, how about Coco?

Dr. Beth: I hate co-co.

Dr. James: Really? Who doesn't like co-co? You can't be that mean.

Dr. Beth: Not with my husband.

Dr. James:
Okay, but you don't know what you're missing.

Dr. Beth keeps walking while Dr. James stood at the other end watching her walk away. She went back downstairs to the basement floor where her office is and a good bit of action is always up for grabs. She walks down the hallway passing a few nurses that are happy to be at work for whatever reason. She got close to the glass doors on the right and a nurse came out looking over a chart.

Dr. Beth: Who's locked down?

Chantell: We have Barbara for observation.

Dr. Beth: Why? What happened?

Chantell: Oh, she had another breakdown.

Dr. Beth wanted to see the chart that Chantell was holding. She opens it up to check the meds that the nurses were giving her.

Dr. Beth: What did you do, give her a higher dose?

Chantell: I did, twenty milligrams.

Dr. Beth: Mmmm, I have to go, that's too much. I need a copy of that on my desk first thing Monday morning okay, Chantell!

Chantell: You got it, doc.

Dr. Beth: Thank you, Chantell.

Dr. Beth walks off. Then she opens the side door to another hallway on the backside of where she and Chantell just spoke about the dosage of medicine that she gave to a patient. She went down three doors to the left into her office. She had a nice sized window with her name on the window pane saying, "Dr. Beth Dickson". She opens the door and walks in. She sits down, going over Amanda's paperwork trying to find a breakthrough. While doing all of that, thunder starts to move in. It made the power go in and out as a few drops of rain hit the ground. Dr. Beth's office is full of work. She has six pictures up of Amanda, Lucy, Barbara, Tammy, Christy, and Melissa. Dr. Beth is thinking to herself as she tries to reach these girls. "The presence of psychotic features reflects severe disease and is a poor prognostic indicator." She sits back and turns on her laptop to look for more answers. Then fourteen seconds later, the power went out, leaving the room in a blackout with no light whatsoever.

Dr. Beth: Shit, damn power. I was getting close.

So she got her bag and overcoat. Then she said, "We'll touch it up later tonight at home." She got up and walked out of her office through the side door. She could barely see as she took short steps, trying not to bump into anything. She saw a light of some kind, so she spoke out.

Dr. Beth: Susan, is that you coming toward me?

Susan: This old ass electric system we got in this damn building gives us trouble every time thunder strikes. I've been telling them that for years. But they always say, "It's too much to replace, ya'll will be ok". Damn cheap fuckers.

Dr. Beth: Two times this week, I'm going for my run.

Susan: Okay, you go do your run. I'm going to do my job. If these old lights would just stay on.

Dr. Beth goes into the locker room. She looks into the mirror and took a deep breath. She closed her eyes for a few seconds. Then she opened them as she sits down. She takes off her shirt and other clothing. Puts on her tights and track shoes. Around and around the track she goes. Then she sat down to catch her breath, relaxing. She then got up to go grab her things and head out. It's been a long day. She goes down the hall toward the front. She sees another guard sitting at the desk watching television. There are cameras in front of him and all over the building to see who's coming and who's not. Dr. Beth walks past the guard.

Dr. Beth: Good night, Trey.

Trey: Hey, young lady, how many laps did you run tonight?

Dr. Beth: 25 laps, and I haven't reached my goal yet.

Trey: Oh, you're improving each time. Be careful, it's a mess out there.

Dr. Beth: Thanks, Trey! Say hi to your lovely wife for me, okay? And tell her I want to try that upside-down peanut butter cake.

Trey: Hahaha!!! I'll make sure I tell her.

Then she walks down three steps and through the front door. She stands there looking at the lightning go across the sky. Then she got herself together and prepared to walk to her car. She looked back at the building which says SANITARIUM PSYCHIATRIC and CORRECTIONAL FACILITY. Dr. Beth got to her car and dropped her keys on the ground. She bent down to reach and picked them up. She stood back up and Dr. James was right behind her. She jumped and hit him in the arm.

Dr. Beth: Boy, you scared the shit out of me.

Dr. James: I'm sorry, I just wanted to see how it felt when Michael Myers did it. I wanted to see how it's done in person.

Dr. Beth: Oh really? Michael Myers? Did you get my text message?

Dr. James: Yeah, yeah, I got your text.

Dr. Beth: Right!!!

Dr. James: I'll follow you home to make sure you get there safely.

Dr. Beth: It's okay, I'm good!

Dr. James: Mmmm, well I suppose to make sure you're good. The boss said so.

Dr. Beth: Oh really? Since when do you follow the boss' orders?

Dr. Beth smiled and got into her car. She shut the door, turned the key, and pulled off. Dr. James quickly followed behind her until she got close. They drove about 3 miles until Dr. Beth turns off on her Street. Dr. James blew the horn as he kept straight on the main road. She turned on the radio station in her car to keep her company while she headed home.

Radio station: Severe showers are coming quickly, as the forecast has it. It should rain all night. Flood warnings until 3 a.m. throughout the state.

Dr. Beth got to a roadblock with four police cars with flashlights and flashers on the side of the road. She stopped and cracked her windows a little. A patrolman walks over and leans over her car to explain.

Policeman: Sorry, ma'am, we can't let you through. The lightning hit a big tree and fell across the road taking down power lines as well.

Dr. Beth: Wow, really?

Then the sheriff got out of the car.

Sheriff: Hey, doc, you picked a bad night to come out. You can't get through, sorry. You're going to have to detour down Old Creek Road by the lake; it's fewer trees but more water.

Dr. Beth: Okay, thanks.

Sheriff: Oh yeah, and tell that busy husband of yours to call me sometimes.

Dr. Beth: You got it. I will let him know.

She backed her car up and took another road to get home to her husband. On her way passing through Old Creek Road, she dropped her cell phone. As she was driving, she was reaching down to pick it up. Trying to keep her eyes on the road at the same time, she looked down twice, then looked back up. She thought she saw a girl standing in the middle of the road. Or was it a deer? She couldn't be sure. She turned the steering wheel to miss what was in the middle of the road. Then she lost control of her car as she took a bad flip into the woods next to the road. She had a cut over her right eye and her nose was bleeding. She tries to get out of the car. She fell to the ground crawling to the main road. She saw a girl standing there with a shirt and pants on no shoes just crying and shaking her head. Dr. Beth stood up and got close to her and got a good look.

Ch. 3
"Face to Face"

Dr. Beth: Who are you? What are you doing out here in the dark in the middle of the road by yourself?

The girl looks at Dr. Beth with tears rolling down her face but still not saying a word. Dr. Beth tries to touch her. The girl moved back and screams. She then passed herself into Dr. Beth's body as the good doctor passes out. Suddenly, she's on the ground. When she opened her eyes, she found herself on the other side with Amanda and the rest of the girls she treated at the facility. She sat up and looked around, waking up in a cold sweat. The lights are blinking off and on. She got up walked to the glass door as if this was a dream. She reaches out to touch it to be sure if it's real or not. Dr. Beth touches the glass door and loses it. She beats on the glass and she yells out for help. Ten minutes later, her good friend, Dr. James, is walking down the hall. Nurse Susan called for him to help calm down Dr. Beth.

Dr. Beth: Nurse Susan, you better tell me what the hell I'm doing caged up like a crazy person!!!!

Susan: Dr. James, hurry, quick, she got up with full power like a wild bull. She was hitting, throwing, kicking, and fighting. Can you get her under control?

Dr. Beth: Bring your ass in here and talk to me.

Dr. James: Hi. Sorry, Susan. I need you to give Dr. Beth a high dose of milligrams.

One of the nurses tries to get Dr. Beth back under control.

Dr. Beth: Get your damn hands off me!!

Dr. James: Relax, Beth, the nurse is just trying to do her job.

Dr. Beth: I'm not playing bitch!

Dr. James: We need a man nurse. Hey, Willie, restrain Beth…she's too much!

Willie went in to restrain Dr. Beth, trying to get her to relax.

Dr. Beth: Keep your hands off. What did I say? Do you think I'm playing games? You hear me? Let me go you, fuckers…NOW!!

Dr. Beth sat down on the bed looking at James shaking her head, upset and mad. You know this ain't right. You know me. I can't believe you and these shitty ass nurses put me in this, locked up, knowing god damn well I don't belong here.

Dr. James: Dr. Beth, if you just relax and let me explain. I'll tell you everything.

Dr. Beth: Okay.

Dr. James: Okay, thank you, nurse!

Susan: Dr. James, are you going to be okay?

Dr. James: Yes!

Dr. Beth: Bitch, take your ass down the hall. He's gonna be okay. Are you okay, bitch?

Dr. James: Beth, please! I'm good, she calmed down.

Nurse Susan shuts the door. "So sad, I feel for Dr. Beth".

Dr. Beth: Okay, Dr. James, start talking.

Dr. James: Beth, this is an eye-opener. Technically, I really shouldn't be treating you. I've spoken to the judge to grant me a short time frame until you get moved. What we say between us is strictly confidential and won't leave these four walls.

Dr. Beth: How long have I been cooped up in this cage?

Dr. James: Two days and one night.

Dr. Beth: Why, James, why?

Dr. James: Beth, at first you were admitted to our neurological unit. You were blacked out. We did scans and they revealed left-sided weakness and numbness. Severe frontal loss deficits. Susan was pumping you with haloperidol when you came. We tested you for drugs and pcp. They were negative. I wanted you to be put in restraints so you wouldn't hurt yourself. Then you slipped into a state of Metafonia.

Dr. Beth: Dr. James, I want to talk to Peter. Tell me, where is he?

Dr. James: Beth, listen to me. You know you're the most logical and outstanding person I know, bar none. And from how you do things, you rely only on facts. I bet you're wondering why I'm telling you all this.

Dr. Beth: You've been keeping up on current personalities. You think I've...well I'm a rational person. You don't think in your heart I'm impulsive or emotional?

Dr. James: It's all about the pattern of analysis. A traumatic event that has rendered this psychological profile useful.

Dr. Beth: You don't think I'm in denial?

Dr. James: Don't analyze yourself. Just focus on remembering.

Dr. Beth leans her head back on the wall in her cell, trying hard to remember everything that took place that day and night. Even until she opened her eyes to the psych ward, she stared off into space for a few.

Dr. James: Beth!!! Open up, let me help you.

She had flashbacks.

Dr. Beth: I remember Amanda earlier. I was having a session with her, trying to get a breakthrough.

Dr. James: What next?

Dr. Beth: She was telling me her dreams. I saw Peter. Plus you were standing in the midst of it. Then I went back to my office and did a little work before the lights started to click off. Then the blackout. I got up to wrap things up. I passed Susan in the hall on the way to run my twenty-five laps. After I got done and was on my way out, I saw Tey and we said goodbye. Then you came and walked me to my car. I turned down the street that I always turn on. The road was blocked. A big tree fell across the road, taking down power lines as well. So I had to take a detour through a back street by the lake.

Dr. James: What happened next? Think hard!

Dr. Beth: I showed up at home. The rain started to come down mixed with ice. I came through the front door and saw Peter. He was pouring himself a drink and watching television in his favorite chair.

Dr. James: Remember. What else, Beth?

Dr. Beth sat there with her eyes glossy. Thoughts racing through her head. She was having a breakthrough. She was driving down a back road by the lake. She thought it was a deer or maybe a girl in the middle of the road when thunder and lightning hit. She tried to turn the wheel fast to avoid hitting what looked to her like a deer or a girl.

Dr. Beth: There was a girl. Now that I think about it! It was a girl…

Dr. James: No, you said there was a deer.

Dr. Beth: No, no, it was a girl.

Dr. Beth stood up so sure of herself that she saw a girl. She also tried to help her. Dr. James stood up.

Dr. James: No, Beth, you thought that. But there was no report of that.

Dr. Beth: The girl was standing there. Big drops of rain was dripping. And she was standing there.

Dr. James: Let's talk about Peter.

They go back and forth about what that was.

Dr. Beth: I'm telling you about this girl and you want to talk about Peter?

Dr. James: Did Dr. Peter ever cheat or beat on you?

Dr. Beth: Are you out of your fucking mind? Hell no. And, and why are you talking about my marriage?

Dr. James: Beth, you don't remember anything about Peter after you saw him when you first walked in? That's all you can tell me?

Dr. Beth: No, please, what do you know about Peter? Did something happen to him?

Dr. James: I have a difficult thing to tell you.

Dr. Beth: No, oh no, don't…

Dr. James: Beth, Peter is dead.

Dr. Beth: NO!

Dr. James: Fingerprints say that you killed him.

She shakes her head. Tears start to fall down her eyes. Suddenly, she yells out, "NO, NO!" Then Dr. James tries to control her, but she's in a rage. She's putting up a fight. He tries to wrap his arms around her and talk her down. She's in shock. Yelling and crying in a rage. He needs help. So he calls out for a male nurse to help him out because Dr. Beth is too much.

Dr. Beth: NO, NO!

Dr. James: A LITTLE HELP HERE!!

Dr. Beth: It wasn't me. You have to believe that it wasn't me. No, no!!

As Dr. Beth cries out in rage saying she didn't do it, Dr. James tries to control her. The male nurse came in to help hold her down. Right behind him was a guard and Susan, the head nurse. They rushed her down to the bed so Susan could give her a shot to relax her and help her sleep.

Dr. James: You'll be okay.

Dr. Beth: It wasn't me, it wasn't me, it wasn't me!

Ch. 4

"I'm Here With You"

Susan: Take it easy, Dr. Beth, we're here for you.

Dr. Beth cries and cries. Now she starts to relax. The male nurse, Susan, and Dr. James began to look like a blur to Dr. Beth. They let her go as she closed her eyes lying down on her back and falling asleep. Two hours later, she woke up. The male nurse came and got her.

Linda: Oh, I see you're up now. Dr. Beth, that's good. Come on time for social hour.

Linda walks Dr. Beth down to the social area with everyone else for her first time. She gets to the sliding door and starts to look around at the other girls. Some she has treated, some she spoke to on day one.

Linda whispered in her ear behind her, "Go ahead, they're not gonna bite".

Ann: Hey look, it's Dr. Dickson.

Amanda looked but had to do a double-take. She couldn't believe it was really Dr. Dickson. Dr. Beth looks at Amanda and then looks away. She started walking over by some chairs by herself and she sat down. Just about everyone was looking at her. She was looking back at them. Amanda saw where her Doctor sat down. Then she got up and started her way over toward Dr. Beth to talk to her.

Amanda: Well, well, this is a turning point. Hello, Beth...

She smiled at Dr. Beth then sat down beside her.

Amanda: Oh, good Doctor, you are one of us now, we are family.

Dr. Beth: I don't belong here, Amanda, you know that.

Amanda: Well, if you here with us, and you got on your wrist band, your gown, and your little socks, oh, I pretty much say that you belong. You're not the big shot doctor in here, and even if you tell the truth, no one is going to believe you. You know why? I'll tell you, good doctor. Because in here, you are CRAZY.

Dr. Beth looks at Amanda and Amanda looks at Dr. Beth and she says, "Coo coo!!

Amanda: Let me give you a tip like you use to give me. The more you try to prove them wrong, saying you don't belong, the crazier you appear. You are one of us, doctor. How are you feeling?

Amanda lies back in the chair looking at Dr. Beth. Then Amanda takes her hand and rubs Dr. Beth on the leg. Dr. Beth pushes her hand away. She tells Amanda not to touch her. Amanda smiles, then whispers to Beth.

Amanda: Are you one of us?

Dr. Beth: NO!

Amanda: You should be.

Then Amanda got up and walked away. The bell rung in four minutes. It was time for them to go back to their cells. Dr. Beth lied down and went back to sleep. Then she woke back up in the dark. The light was blinking off and on. She woke up in a cold sweat and looking around. She sat up in her bed breathing heavily and looking straight at the glass door. Dr. Beth got up and just stood there looking at the glass, like something was there. She heard a bump on the door but no one was there. Then fog appeared on the glass, spelling out, "I'm here with you". Then it disappeared like smoke in thin air. Dr. Beth started to look scared. She has worry written all over her face and spreading through her eyes. She felt something go past her. She trusts that she felt nothing. Then she felt it again. She turned and saw nothing again. Dr. Beth starts to walk back to her bed, talking to herself, saying, "It's not real, it's like a logical dream, that's all, nothing else. It's not real, the whispers, the fog on the glass. No way, I'm tripping". She sat down on her bed, shaking her head, and repeatedly saying, "It's not real".

Dr. Beth: No, not happening, not real, I'm not crazy!

She stayed balled up on her bed so long that she didn't even know it was a new day. Then Susan,

Susan's assistant, and one guard stood by her door as Susan touched her on the head.

Susan: Up, up, up, it's a new day, sugar!

Dr. Beth: I wanna have a word with Dr. James.

Susan: In due time, honey. You'll get to see Dr. James. But right now, it's time for you to take your pills. Breakfast is the most important round here.

Dr. Beth: I think I'll pass on them pills you have in your hand. Why are you treating me like this, Susan?

Susan: Sugar, I have to do my job. Come on and take your pills. You don't want me to call Larry in here to help you now, do you?

Dr. Beth looks at Susan and grabbed the cup of pills. Then she took them and drank water behind it. She gave the cup back to Susan.

Dr. Beth: What?

Susan: You know, open wide.

As Susan ensured Dr. Beth has taken her medicine, she moves on.

Susan: Now, see, that wasn't too bad after all, good girl. Oh, get up, sweetheart. It's time to go get your blood drawn. Up, up, up!

Dr. Beth walks into the room with eight other girls. Beth stood at the door like she didn't want to go in.

Susan: Oh, come on, Beth, it's time to face the facts.

Dr. Beth was in the crowd as they talked amongst themselves. Dr. Beth saw something. She's looking at all the girls look back at her and whisper stuff. It seems like they're talking about her but she can't make out what they're saying. Dr. Beth closed her eyes and rubbed her face slowly. She's trying to clear her mind and take a few deep breaths. She heard something that made her gasp and open her eyes (like mmmm, she's nuts). She looks around and the voices pick up. "Yeah, it's you". She turns and looks to see Amanda smiling at her. Then the whispers start to get louder. She looks through the crowd. She then wonders if she'll see the girl that she saw that night by the lake, standing there looking at her with killer eyes. She yells scarily, then hides behind a girl. She's looking back to see if the girls were still there where she saw her before. She turned away and hid behind another girl. She looked and no one was there, but Amanda was closer to her than she was before. She looks another way because she heard the whispers. Dr. Beth is starting to freak out. Voices are getting clear. "You should run". Dr. Beth hid behind another girl in fear. It feels like someone is after her in that crowd of girls. Then Amanda started to walk. Like what's going on? Dr. Beth moved away from one girl and bumped into Amanda in fear.

Amanda: Hey, what is your problem?

She turned and looked. The voices are getting louder. She turned and her eyes got big. Her mouth was wide open. She's looking around, bumping into the other girls. She's scared out of her mind. She turned one way and she saw Jennifer. She looked the other way. She looked one way and saw Jennifer anyway. She is freaking out. She turned back and she saw her face to face. Dr. Beth yells. To her, it seems like the girls are taking a knife and cutting on her.

She can feel the cuts. No one can see why she is yelling. She fell on the floor. Everyone starts to run over her and to one side of the room. Dr. Beth drops down and balled up crying on the floor. From where she's laying, the guard and Susan came and picked her up. They took her to a room and got her all cleaned up. They sat her on the bed so they could treat her for the cuts that she got. No one knows how she got them.

Ch. 5
"WHY?"

Susan: I was talking to one of the other nurses. I had my back turned and what I did was unacceptable.

Dr. James: Susan, it's not your fault. Patients tend to find a way to hurt themselves if that's what they want.

Susan: I never thought Dr. Beth would be a cutter. I really didn't.

Dr. James: Me either. I'm pretty shocked at what I've been seeing coming from the doctor.

Susan: Barbara said Amanda has been coming after Dr. Beth. So I've decided to put her in isolation for two days.

Dr. James: So, doctor, how is Dr. Beth?

Dr. Randy: Not so good. I can't believe she's gone so quickly. It's the damnest thing I've ever seen. She cut herself fourteen times. To me, that's superficial.

Dr. James: Implement?

Dr. Randy: Probably a scalpel or a sharp object. I don't know how anyone could get that past the guards. I really don't.

Dr. Beth sat on the bed by herself. Then stands up and walks over to the mirror and stares at the cut on her face. She has this blank look about her that's stiff as a tree branch in the winter. The door opened. She looked to see who's walking in the room. She sees that it's Dr. James. He walks in and told Beth to please come to have a seat so they can talk. She walks over and sat down. Dr. James asked to see Beth's other arm so he could look at them. Then he asked her to open her mouth to take her temperature. She just looked at him and said, "Please". Then she opened up. A few minutes went by. He wrote something on the chart.

Dr. Beth: So, doc, do you think I've done this to myself?

Dr. James: Mmmm, did you?

Dr. Beth: No! Do you think I would?

Dr. James: Mmmm, I can't say. I'm not so sure. So who would it be? You tell me.

Dr. Beth: You're the doctor.

Dr. James: Did Amanda do it or....?

Dr. Beth: I really don't know, James.

Dr. James: Well, you know, Beth, you have difficulty distinguishing what's reality from fantasy. So you tell me, help me help you.

Dr. Beth: You know, as a doctor, I can understand why you would think that. But overall, being on both sides, a doctor and a patient, something is really going on with me, I do know that.

Dr. James: I see! Tell me, is this a hallucination?

Dr. Beth: You tell me!

Dr. James: How do you feel about me increasing your medication until what you're going through starts to make sense?

Dr. Beth: Or maybe I need a new doctor. How do you feel about that?

Dr. James: Why?

Dr. Beth: Since I'm "hallucinating" and I can't remember things as you say. How about you help me with something.

Dr. James: Oh yeah? (Inhale)

Dr. Beth: Do you have a thing for me?

Dr. James rubbed his eyes' and took a deep breath.

Dr. James: Yes!

Dr. Beth: Did you want to take me to bed?

Dr. James: Yes.

Dr. Beth: Do you think I felt the same way you felt for me?

Dr. James: Yes!

Dr. Beth: So why didn't it ever happen?

Dr. James: Because you were married to the boss.

Dr. Beth: And now?

A few tears drop from Dr. Beth' eyes.

Dr. James: I'm a doctor. We're on two different sides. I'm….well, I'm trying to help you, trust me.

He grabbed her hands and looked her dead in the eyes'.

Dr. Beth: But why should I trust a person who thinks I'm crazy?

Dr. James let's go of her hands. He sat back taking a breath. Then he got up and walked out of the room, leaving her with her thoughts and tears. Two days later, the guards open the doors for the girls to get some fresh air outside. They walked in a single file line, one by one. Each one of them stepped onto the outside soil. Dr. Beth was in that line up as she saw Dr. Allie Mae (chief of the board of doctors). She calls out to her at the gate. Dr. Allie was on her way to her car.

Dr. Beth: Allie!!!!!

Allie Mae: Hello, Beth.

Dr. Beth: May I have a moment of your time?

The old doctor stopped walking and looked at Beth. She stated that this is about Dr. James. Allie walks over to the gate to hear Beth out.

Dr. Allie: Okay, you may have your say. Tell me, what about him?

Dr. Beth: I don't think he is the right doctor to be treating me at this point.

Dr. Allie: Is your complaint about Dr. James personally or…?

She shakes her head no.

Dr. Allie: Dr. James is the top doctor that I have on my staff. I support him one-hundred percent. Now I hope I was helpful to you. If you will excuse me, I'll be on my way.

She just looked at Dr. Beth then walked away. Dr. Beth looked back at Allie and stood there thinking no one is on her side. Her back is against the wall.

The next morning, a nurse came to get Beth from her cell. The family lawyer was there to see her. Susan will escort her down to visit with him. Dr. Beth and nurse Susan opened the door to the visitors, one in one room with a desk and four chairs. Her lawyer, Dave Parker, was waiting on her to arrive. Now they can discuss what's going on with the case and when she will get out of that cell.

Dave Parker: Hello, Beth.

Dr. Beth: Hi, Dave.

She hugged Dave real tight. Didn't want to let him go. She knew that they needed to talk about the case.

Ch. 6
"Evidence"

Nurse Susan just stood behind her and smiled.

Dave Parker: How are you holding up? Are they treating you okay?

Dr. Beth: Dave, they are treating me like I'm crazy. They think I killed Peter. No one is on my side. I really didn't do it, I really....

Dave Parker: Okay, okay, let's have a seat. Thank you, nurse, that will be all.

Susan said, "I'll be right over here if you need me". Then she walked away.

Dr. Beth and Dave sat across from each other at the table.

Dave Parker: Let's not talk about what you did and didn't do at this point. What I want to talk about is what I can do for you at this point. Now the D.A. is pressing for a hearing sometime next week.

Dr. Beth: What the fuck, what the hell! There's been no time for an investigation, you know that, Dave.

Dave Parker: Understand, Beth, as your attorney, I must say that the evidence is heart-stopping. You've been appointed at the scene. The sheriff said that you were on your way home that night. One or two neighbors said they saw you pull up at a time not too long after the sheriff told you and gave you the time. Evidence has your prints all over the murder weapon that they got from the house, your home, Beth. They took samples from the walls and the floor. They all read your prints.

Dr. Beth: I hear you, Dave, come on. You know me. What's my motive? I don't have one. Why would I kill my husband? I love him. We got along and everything. Just like best friends. Maybe someone that's been hunting for him for a long time did it. Now that person would have a motive. Yes, I was there. I'm telling you, Dave, I did not kill Peter, no way.

Dave Parker: Beth, the only way I think we should go is to plead temporary insanity. Hell, I don't even know if they would believe that. Because you are a gifted and smart psychiatrist; maybe it'll turn the jurors into thinking, "Hey, if she wanted to kill someone she'd probably fake insanity and win". This, this is the sweet part about it…and get away with it. Do you understand what I'm saying?

Dr. Beth: I'm telling you, I'm not this crazy person that people think I am.

Dave Parker: That's the idea.

Dr. Beth: No, no, damn that. The idea is I'm the only person around here that really believes I didn't kill Peter! Is it sinking in, Dave?

She looked at Dave eye to eye as if she has nothing to lose for about ten seconds.

Dr. Beth: Look me in my eyes, Dave, and tell me, do you think I'm crazy?

Dave looked at Beth. He could barely look at her. It was written all over his face that she is crazy. So Beth slammed her hand down real hard on the table then sat back in the chair.

Dr. Beth: Got dammit, that's what I thought. Forget it.

She puts her hand on her face and starts to rub her face to try and relax. Her own attorney looks like he doesn't believe her and that's the last hope she was counting on.

Dave Parker: Look, Sheriff Thomas is in the building and he wants to speak with you as well. He and Peter grew up together. I advise against it.

Beth put her hands down and looked at her attorney.

Dr. Beth: It's okay, Dave. Let him speak.

Dave Parker asked the sheriff to come and sit with Dr. Beth and him. The guard waved to the other guard to let the sheriff in. He walks in and pulled him up a chair. Dr. Beth was looking at him wondering what's on his mind. What do you have to say? The sheriff got beside the attorney.

Then Dr. Beth looked back and saw Dr. James. He moved his lips, staring at Dr. Beth with no sound. "Three minutes max". The sheriff and Dr. Beth looked at each other for twenty seconds.

Dr. Beth: Hi, Thomas.

Sheriff Thomas: Beth! I won't be long. I just have a few questions I want to ask. When you first walked into the house and you saw Peter, did you strike him from behind or in front? Did he see it coming or was he surprised? What I don't understand is how he…Damn this, why did you do it, Beth?

Dave Parker: No, sheriff!

Sheriff Thomas: You just killed Peter like he was a deer. He loved you more than life itself. Tell me, please. Why did you? Now answer that.

Dave Parker: Beth, you don't have to answer.

Dr. Beth: I don't have any answers, Thomas, I really don't.

Sheriff Thomas: Oh, you don't? Well, miss big-time doctor, you better come up with something because you're in deep trouble.

Dr. James: Sheriff, that's not how we do things. You are out of line, that's enough.

Sheriff Thomas: No, no, not nearly enough. Tell me, Beth.

Dr. James: Okay, we are done, no more!

Sheriff Thomas: Not even close to being done. Let's see how you like it if your childhood best friend got killed.

Dr. James: You said you were not going over the top and then you get out of line.

Sheriff Thomas: Out of line? I'll show you out of line.

So the sheriff turned on his tablet with pictures of the crime scene. Blood everywhere. Stab wounds to Peter's chest, arms, back, and stomach.

Dr. James: Cut that off sheriff. Why would you show her that stuff?

Dave Parker: Beth, don't look at them.

Dr. Beth was going through the pictures. Swiping the screen side to side. She's in shock that there is so much blood.

Sheriff Thomas: See, I had to put him in a body bag, my good buddy.

She lifted her head up, shaking and looking at everyone.

Dr. Beth: I didn't do this. Really, I didn't do this.

The lawyer looked at her face. On the left side, she had a patch. He asked her, "What is that?"

She took the bandage off because she can feel blood leaking on her face.

Dave Parker: Beth, what's wrong with your face?

She took the patch off her face and it read: "I'm Here With You!"

As she looks at everyone, Dr. James, Sheriff Thomas, and Dave was looking in shock. She flipped the screen. She saw I'm here with you on the front door of her home and the backside. Dr. Beth stood up looking at them.

Susan: Hey, it's okay. Relax, Beth.

Dr. Beth: What's going on with me?

Susan: Dr. Beth, relax, we're all done.

Dr. James and Susan just tried to restrain Beth. She's looking at her attorney and the sheriff as they stand there staring at her with blank looks on their faces. She takes a few steps backward and cries. Susan tells her, "It's okay". Dr. James got her strapped to a bed so she could relax without putting up a fight. Susan wrapped Beth's face back up on the one side, keeping it fresh. Then both of them left her so she could rest.

Her eyes' are closed. She moves her head side to side for a little bit, back and forth as she goes into a deep dream. Thinking of how things unfolded. She saw visions of cutting Peter. Then visions of Peter losing a lot of blood. The whole hand covered as he tries to crawl up the stairs. Then she saw parts of her taking a cloth and wiping it on Peter's back where he's losing a lot of blood. She's writing "I'm Here With You" on the wall. Then flashes of him yelling, "WHY?!" Then flashes of what she had on that night. She saw the knife that she picked up in the kitchen.

Then she had a flash on going out of the side door to the main road, walking as rain and ice comes down. Then flashes of her walking back down the road by the lake where she saw Jennifer standing there, crying with a t-shirt on. No shoes and no pants. Her eyes' opened up, then rolled back into her head. Her head was shaking back and forth. Flashes of Jennifer crying in front of her. Then she got a clear look at what she looked like before she got into Dr. Beth's body. She is possessed. Now she's seen it all. Now she can take matters into her own hands. The next day, she asks to see Allie Mae. She and Dr. James walked into her office. Dr. James knocked on the door. Allie looked up to see who it was.

Ch. 7
"That Night"

Allie Mae: Come in!

The door opened. Dr. Beth and Dr. James were standing there.

Allie Mae: Well, come in, come in. Don't just stand there.

Dr. Beth walks in looking at Allie. She tells her to have a seat. From the looks of it, it seems like Dr. Beth has been crying all night and she looks pretty worn out.

Allie Mae: Beth, I hear you wanted to see me.

Dr. Beth: Yes, I was at my house the night it all went down. I was there when Peter got killed as well as when he was alive.

Allie Mae shook her head and agreed with Beth.

Dr. Beth: But the strange thing about it is, I wasn't alone.

Allie Mae: What do you mean, Beth?

Dr. Beth: I wasn't alone. That's what "I'm here with you" means.

Dr. James looked at Dr. Beth as she starts to shed more tears. She's trying to get her words out.

Dr. James: Who was there?

Dr. Beth: I really don't know who it was. I don't know, I don't know!! I tell you the truth, somebody else was there.

Dr. James: Allie!

Allie: Beth, we know Peter was all you had. No children and your mom and dad died when you were four years old. We are your family. Now you've been like a daughter to me.

She dropped her head and broke down.

Dr. Beth: I know, I know, I know…

Allie Mae: I really need you to understand that we are going to do everything in our power to help you and make sure you feel secure. I hope you can trust us as your family.

Dr. Beth stopped crying and started to stare at a picture that Allie Mae has on her table behind her of a young girl. A photo of the same girl she's been seeing in her dreams. In the night, she gets up out of the chair. Dr. James tries to grab her arm but she pulls away from him so she can walk over to see that photo on the table. Dr. James and Allie Mae stood up.

Allie Mae: What is it, Beth?

Dr. James: Please sit down. Come on, Beth!

She got a closer look as she picked up the photo. She stared at it.

Dr. Beth: Tell me, who is this girl? She's the one I've been seeing all this time.

Dr. James: Please put it back.

Dr. Beth: NO!! Stop. Who is she?

Allie Mae: The girl in the picture that you are holding in your hand is my daughter, Jennifer.

Dr. James: Give Allie the picture, Beth.

Dr. Beth: No, no, not yet. This is the same girl I've been seeing in my dreams at night. This is the girl!

Dr. James: She looks like someone you have been dreaming about, but you don't know her.

Dr. Beth: This is her.

Allie Mae: It can't be her, Beth.

Dr. Beth: How is she? Where is she? Let me see her.

Allie Mae: There's no way you could see her.

Dr. Beth: This is her, I swear!

Allie Mae: Dr. Beth, Jen is dead!!

Dr. Beth froze. She looked shocked.

Allie Mae: Jennifer died there years ago, the day after tomorrow.

She looked at the picture before she put it down. Dr. James took her back to her room. Hours went by. Darkness has set upon them. The lights are going out. The place is so quiet you can hear a pin drop. A cold chill crossed the hallway. The lights start blinking on and off. Dr. Beth doesn't know it as she is in a deep sleep. Wet footprints walk up the hall, step by step, passing one glass door, two glass doors, three glass doors, then four glass doors, and the footprints stopped at the fifth door. Then they faced Dr. Beth's glass door, standing there as she sleeps. Dr. Beth sat up on her bed, pushing the covers off of her. She looked straight ahead thinking she saw something.

Dr. Beth: I'm a rational person by far. I believe things happen for a reason. But I don't believe in the paranormal, or ghosts. I have a question. If you are the ghost of Jennifer Mae, unlock this cell door and I can walk out of here.

Four seconds after saying that, Dr. Beth's cell door opened up and was cracked for Beth to come out. She got up off her bed and put both feet on the cold floor with no socks on, just some loose pants and a short-sleeved shirt. She takes her time as she walks toward the glass door. She then takes the palm of her hands and pushed the heavy glass door open. She steps out of the cell looking toward the right side of the hall to see if someone was down there. She started to walk that way as well. Then she took a look behind her as she continues to jog to the sliding doors. She gets to the sliding and peeks out of them, making sure the coast is clear. She steps out on the other side of the sliding doors, closing them behind her, and feeling a cool breeze blow her hair. She quickly turns and looks down the hallway to see the girl she has been seeing. She was walking in that room with those pants and a shirt and with no shoes and socks on. She was looking at her, but Dr. Beth can't see her face as she walks. It freaks her out, as Dr. Beth's eyes got big. Her mouth wide open but nothing is coming out. She starts moving in the other direction away from Jennifer. She starts to run looking back towards time, making sure she's not following her.

She sees a guard across the end of the hall talking on his walky-talky and walking from one end to the other, making his rounds. She puts on the breaks and falls flat on her ass. She got back up on her feet as fast as she hit her ass on the floor. She scaled a wall behind the door to take over. A cleaning woman opened the door from the other side. She pushed the door back to where Beth was. She was coming out with a housekeeper's cart until another woman said to her, "Lisa, do you need more trash bags?" Lisa walked back into the room, leaving the cart bracing the door as Beth pokes her head from behind the door, looking in Lisa's cart for anything sharp to open a door or crack a window. She picked up a scraper off the cart and ran back the other way. Down the hall, she got to a door that was locked and turned the scraper around and broke out a big enough hole in the window of the door to stick her hand out the other side to unlock it so she could go through it. She sticks her arm through and unlocked the door. She got to the other side. She realizes this hallway is the one her and Dr. James' offices are on. Beth heads toward them. She quickly ran to her office. It was locked and empty, only a desk and two chairs.

Dr. Beth: Damn, they cleaned me out. Oh, Dr. James' office.

She looked next door in Dr. James' office. It was locked. She took the scraper and popped the lock to get in. She pushed the door back up once she got in. She made her way to his desk. She tried to open his desk and it was locked. So she took the scraper and popped the lock to get in it. She got it opened and got his keys out of it. She pushed the drawer back up and started to walk away. The computer turns on and it is showing a clip of Jennifer committing suicide by drowning in a lake (Daily news). The local sheriff says this must have occurred late that evening or at night when visibility is poor. She should have been able to make it on her own. A police autopsy indicates that there was no foul play. Alcohol and drugs were not a factor. It is believed that the extent of the damage is that the girl slipped and fell into the lake. Seconds later, Jennifer's body popped up on the screen looking dead into the video so Dr. Beth can see her as the background show. The lights are starting to blink on and off like they have a shortage in them. Beth realized what hall Jennifer had been staying on. It was the same one as Amanda's. She quickly got up to go to that hallway. "SOLITARY!"

Dr. Beth: Amanda!!

Dr. Beth made a copy of what she saw on the screen. She folded the paper up, then put it in her back pocket. She runs out of the office down to the hallway and through the double doors that read: "Strictly Authorized Personnel Only". She went through them anyway. Then she came to another set of doors. It led her right to Amanda's hall (RESTRICTED AREA. DANGER!). The lights are blinking off and on, which means she's there or Jennifer is close. Dr. Beth takes sixteen steps down the middle of the hall until she heard a loud thump. It was so loud that it made Dr. Beth jump. She turned toward a door where she thought the noise came from. She walks a little closer to get a better listen. Then Amanda's face hits the glass hard, making Beth jump back. There's a cut over Amanda's right eye. Beth takes off running through the same doors that she came in. She's yelling out, "HELP, SOMEBODY HELP ME" as she runs through the hallways. She ran into Susan at full speed, knocking Susan down and the tray she was carrying. The medicines on the tray went everywhere. Larry and Paul were walking behind Susan and talking amongst themselves about what had happened the last few seconds of the baseball game the other night. They grabbed Beth, trying to hold her down. She's kicking and yelling: "Check on Amanda, she's in trouble!" Let me go, let me go. A few minutes later, they had Beth in a locked cage like the one she and Amanda were in from the start. The head nurse, Susan, called Dr. James to come see about Dr. Beth. She's pacing back and forth. The guards are looking at the monitors, keeping a close eye on Beth, still wondering how she got out of her cell in the first place.

Dr. James walked in and waves at everyone. He then took his keys out of his pocket and unlocked the one gate. He walked in and Beth saw him coming. She stood by the door at the other gate she was being held. He walked up to it and put his key in to unlock the room she was in.

Ch. 8
"The Talk"

Dr. Beth: Did you speak with Amanda?

Dr. James: I did!

Dr. James stepped inside that cage with Dr. Beth to have a little chat about what's going on.

Dr. Beth: Was she hurt?

Dr. James: Huh, hurt a little. Why?

Dr. Beth: Did you check her out all over?

Dr. James: Did I? Beth, she was checked within the standards of our field of work.

Dr. Beth: It didn't have time...

Dr. James: It? What do you mean it?

Dr. Beth: Did you check her face? She hit the door. I mean the glass part. I saw blood running down her face.

Dr. James: Ummmm, she ran into the door.

Dr. Beth: Really, ran into the door and you believe it?

Dr. James: She did it to herself.

Dr. Beth: I saw a man's chest with scars on it. Did she say anything about that?

Dr. James: Come on. Let's sit down. Scars, huh?

Dr. Beth: Yea, deep scars.

Dr. James: Are you sure?

Dr. Beth: I know what I saw!

Dr. James: It's common something flashed quickly in front of your eyes. You may think you saw something.

Dr. Beth: I'm not talking about a thought. I'm talking about something I saw on a man's chest.

Dr. James: You good?

Dr. Beth: That's what I saw.

Dr. James: That image is tailor-made for your state of mind. A man in the cell with Amanda.

Dr. James opened up his jacket pocket and pulled out a copy of Jennifer that Dr. Beth had in her hand when she took off running out of those doors and when she saw Susan, Larry, and Paul as they were trying to hold her down.

Dr. James: I need you to explain this to me.

Dr. Beth: Jennifer Mae did not commit suicide.

Dr. James: She slipped off the bridge.

Dr. Beth: No, when I saw her…

Dr. James: She was washed down the stream.

Dr. Beth: She had so many cuts on her.

Dr. James: You saw Jennifer? What does that mean?

Dr. Beth: Yes, I did. Someone did that to her.

Dr. James: Ummm, newspapers, local police are all wrong. Is that what you're saying?

Dr. Beth: She was beaten up!

Dr. James: Really? Let's reopen the case.

Dr. Beth: They should, that's a start. I'm telling you, I saw Jennifer. When she touched me we connected.

Dr. James: Delusions, hallucinations, disorganized.

Dr. Beth: How? I don't know.

Dr. James: Incoherence.

Dr. Beth: Hey, hey, hey, don't run that psychiatric bullshit on me, James. I know that shit like the first day of school.

Dr. James: OKAY! OKAY! Fine, that way I don't have to sit here and go through the chain of steps.

Dr. James got up and walked to the door and unlocked it. He stepped out and locked it back behind him while looking at Dr. Beth.

Dr. James: That cell you were staying in with the glass doors is having electrical problems. It's something, but they haven't got down to the bottom of it yet. I got you transferred to the psych ward. They're watching you, so don't give me a reason. If you blow this, I have no choice but to put you in solitary.

Dr. James starts to walk off.

Dr. Beth: Jennifer Mae was really there. Ghost or alive, I don't know. She was there and she came to me for a reason.

The next morning, everyone was outside for some fresh air as the guards looked on. It's a rather cool and breezy morning. The clouds thickened up and the smell of rain was in the air. Who could tell at this given time? The heat barely comes this way, just a cool breeze. Some come in to bond with each other. Others come out to get some fresh air. Dr. Beth was last to come out in the yard. She walks with her arms crossed as the wind blew so lightly through her hair as she walks into the wind. She looked for Amanda and she walked toward her, seeing her just looking off without a care in the world. Dr. Beth sat down by Amanda.

Dr. Beth: Hi, Amanda! I'm here for you. I'm really sorry for not believing in you. I need you to tell me who did that to you. Tell me, you can trust me.

Amanda smiled, looking at Dr. Beth face to face.

Dr. Beth: Tell me, Amanda, tell me anything.

Amanda: I'll tell you this. He can touch me, rape my body, but one thing for sure he'll never have is my soul. You understand, doc. NEVER!!!

Then Amanda looks back straight into the wind. Dr. Beth stood up and looked into the wind, then she looked back at Amanda. Dr. Beth turns away from Amanda with her back towards her, thinking to herself. "What the hell is going on?" She thinks. Then Amanda stood up. Beth turns to face her. Amanda then reaches out and hugged her tight. They both look scared.

Dr. Beth: It will be alright, Amanda, it will be alright.

Amanda put her mouth by Dr. Beth's ear and whispered.

Amanda: He told me you're next!

She looked into the sky with thoughts crossing her mind. Later that day, as night falls, the nurses are on duty hard. They are short-staffed. Susan walks through the door talking to another nurse that was at the desk catching up on paperwork.

Susan: Hey, nurse, drink you some coffee. I need you tonight.

Ch. 9
Something Is Wrong

Nurse: Yes, ma'am

Then Susan went out of another door. On the other side of the nurse, she put her key in and opened it. She stepped through before closing the door. She walked down the hall and she told the nurse.

Susan: If you need me, I'll be in the lady's room. Then I will make my way to the coffee station.

She started down the hallway, step by step until she got to door number nine. She went over and took a peek inside the small glass checking on Dr. Beth. In a lockdown, she is at the other end of the bed, sitting there in deep thought with her head down. Susan hit the buzzer on the wall to the nurse that she just saw and told her.

Susan: Lights out on this hall.

As Dr. Beth sits there, the light from the small window grazed across her face as she sat facing the wall and a three-layer bookshelf, sitting on her bed with a blanket and pillow with just enough space to move around. Dr. Beth lifted her head up because she thought she heard something. The lights outside her cell started to blink off and on. She knew now Jennifer was close. The light stopped blinking. She turns around and looks over her right shoulder, then back at the door, slowly, step by step, and with worry on her face. She stopped and peeked out of the window. She sees nothing. Then her eye catches a shadow and moves by the base of the door where it's very little light shining through. She dropped down. Behind her is Jennifer looking down at her. She felt something. Dr. Beth stood up quickly and turned around to see what it is. No one was there. But the inside of the room was shaking. She walked back toward the other end of the room looking at the walls and the light that's on the ceiling, then looking behind her as she turns around slowly. She is thinking to herself, "What the hell is going on?" She turned and looked. The light flashes off and on faster and faster. Then she hears a sound. She turns back around and sees Jennifer face to face with a mad look on her face. Dr. Beth yelled. Jennifer pushed Beth up in the air to the other side of the room, hitting her head on the wall as she falls to the bed and onto the floor, flipping her bed on top of her. She got up quickly, scared out of her mind. Her back was up against the wall, eyes wide open, looking toward the other end of the room where she got thrown from.

Dr. Beth: Why are you doing this to me?

Jennifer grabbed Beth by the throat, choking her. Then she threw her into the bookshelf, head first. Her feet were up in the air. The bookshelf was broken into pieces as she dropped to the floor. The two guards on that floor were looking at the western "Gun Smoke" and all the cameras in the rooms. They were not looking at them because, at this time, they are either asleep or just lying in their beds.

Guard: Aah, man, that old man knew he didn't have a chance against a young, fast gunfighter.

Guard 2: Hell, maybe he thought he had a chance.

Guard: Hahahaha! Hey, look over there at cell nine, Dr. Beth is trying to kill herself.

The guard pointed to the screen on cell nine. The second guard got up and walked over to the screen.

Guard 2: What the fuck?!

Guard: Look at that! See how she's throwing herself against the wall side by side.

Guard 2: Get on the walkie. I'm going out there.

Guard: Level three, we got suicidal behavior in cell nine. Bring back up ASAP!

He ran down the stairs to the gate where the nurses are.

Guard 2: Open up quickly, open up!!!

The nurse buzzed the doors open. The guard didn't have to use the key. He ran through the doors and down the hallway. Susan was running down the other end of the hall. She was meeting the guard to see what was going on.

Guard 2: Hey, Susan, Dr. Beth is bouncing off the walls!!

The guard yelled out, "Open up cell nine", as he looks inside. They open the door.

Susan: Oh My God!!!

Dr. Beth is lying face down on the floor. The room is broke down, flipped upside down, as they stepped inside.

Guard 2: Look at this. What a mess.

Susan: Sit her up. I want to medicate her.

Guard 2: Shit, Susan, for what? She's already knocked out.

Susan: Don't mouth back at me. Just do it!

Guard two reached down to see if she's dead or alive. He put his hand on her pulse. Dr. Beth sat up quickly, pushed him against the wall, smacking his head on the wall and knocking him out. She then put Susan up on the wall by the throat. Susan held up her hands begging her.

Susan: Please! Easy, easy, don't kill me!

Dr. Beth took Susan's keys off of her side. She ran out of the room and down the hall toward the gate where the nurses sit.

Susan: Hey, stop her, she's got my keys!

Ch. 10
"The Close Escape"

Nurse: Shit, oh shit!

The nurse got up trying to shut the gate coming from behind her desk. Beth is running at top speed like a running back. She's not thinking about stopping. The nurse almost got the gate closed. Beth runs into the gate with full force. She knocked the nurse backward over a chair onto the floor. Now she's knocked out. Beth got through the first gate. Then the second gate. She goes through a room. She then takes the keys that she got off of Susan and unlocked the cell door with bars on it. The guard saw her come in. He's upstairs yelling, "She's free!"

Guard: Hold it right there!

Dr. Beth kept running toward another cell door. He got on his walkie talkie.

Guard: Dr. Beth is running!! She's escaping level three!

He goes after her. She ran upstairs. Then another gate. He loses sight of her as he opened the gate. He got up the stairs. She ran through more guards. Then they meet up.

Guard 5: There she is. She's going to level seven!

She climbed up and got to the top. Then she opened the hatch and made her way back up another set of stairs. The keys were in her mouth while she looked around for an exit. She got to the top and saw two doors. She ran to the black door on her left.

Dr. Beth: SHIT!!

Then she ran back across the room to the other door, a brown door on her right. It barely opened up. She squeezed through it. She's walking trying to find a way out, looking down as she walks. Then she runs into a dead end with nowhere to go.

Dr. Beth: Shit, trap!

She looked and looked and found a small opening in the fence like an old jail used to be. She looked back. The guards are trying to get through the door she had trouble with.

Guard 5: Hey, stop! Let us help you!

She squeezed through the fence. From the looks of it, it's about two, maybe three levels high. Dr. Beth started to climb down, taking easy steps and hoping she doesn't fall. She could still hear the voices from the guards.

Guard 1: She's on the upper level!

She lost her grip sliding down the fence. She held on with her hands.

Dr. Beth: Damn! That was close.

The guards got there. They ran to the end of the walkway where Dr. Beth got out.

Guard 3: Hold it, doc.

One of the guards got their walkie talkie.

Guard 6: We're on the top floor. She's headed for the first floor.

She dropped, lost her grip, and falls to the floor on her back, just about knocking the wind out of her. She was slow to get up. She made a face like (damn that shit hurt). She shook it off and started to run to the other end of the hall. She passed some things that use to be useful. Old chairs, tables, and beds all piled up with dust and spider webs. She found her way back to a place that she knew all too well—the gym she used to work out in while she was working there. She ran toward the sliding doors. Then she saw men walking and talking with flashlights. She stopped and looked at the men's locker room and she went in. She headed to the back of the shower and saw this glass room. It had a mini pool in it. The voices are getting louder and coming near her. She has to think quickly. She ducked down peaking to see where the two guards are. She saw the lights coming from their flashlights (the main lights are out). She tried another door and it's locked. She looked around then dipped into the mini pool, slowly and easily into it because the water is so cold.

Guard: Hey, Billy boy, let's check the pool in the locker rooms.

Billy: Sure thing, buddy.

Guard: She might be in here, maybe not.

Billy: She, mmmm, we'll see.

Guard: Yeah, we're all over this building. Don't know where she could go.

Dr. Beth dropped down deep into the pool holding her breath. This is the longest she ever held it, three minutes and twenty-five seconds flat.

Billy: Dr. Beth is smart!

Guard: She's not that smart if we catch her.

Billy: I'm glad she's on the run; hell, I was falling asleep like a boring man.

Guard: Hell, the longer we look the more overtime we get.

Billy: All you think about is money.

Guard: Hey, it makes the world go round.

The guards go into the glass room where the pool is. They shined the lights in there to see what they could see. Dr. Beth stayed under the water as they passed by making their way out.

Billy: Come on, let's go, she's not in here.

Dr. Beth closed her eyes and was trying to go off of sounds to see when the guard was leaving before she came up for air. They went out of the side door. Then she opened up her eyes and the ghost of Jennifer was looking right back at her. She screamed under the water rushing to get to the top. She jumped out of the pool standing against the wall, barely breathing and trying to catch her breath.

Dr. Beth: OK!! OK!!

The guards were walking towards the front entrance talking amongst themselves.

Guard 3: We checked corridors top and bottom.

Guard: It's okay, we're going to check the labs. Is Trey at the front desk?

Guard: What's going on? It's dark as fuck. I woke up and no lights.

Guard: What do you mean what do I mean?

Trey is at the desk trying to get the lights turned back on.

Trey: Look, this stuff has happened a few times this month. Get these lights on, my guards are walking around with flashlights.

Person on the phone: Hey, buddy, chill out. I'm trying to get them back on.

Trey: Yea, it's about time!! Thank you!!

Person on the phone: Finally.

They both hung up the phone.

Dr. Beth is walking on her hands and knees dripping wet, sliding up under Tey's desk. Tey then looked down.

Trey: Oh shit!

She's trying to whisper, "Please don't give me up", but no words were coming out.

Guard 1: Hey, Trey, what do you see?

Trey: Yeah, oh yeah. Just then the monitors turned back on with the lights. I thought I saw a shadow on the top floor. Something flashed in front of the camera.

Guard 1: Okay, Larry, you take the east stairs. Danny, you take the west stairs. Get back to me on the walkie talkie and let me know what you see when you get there. Come on, people, move!

Everyone cleared out. Trey looked back down at Dr. Beth under his desk. She wrote, "I need a way out of here please".

Trey: Here, take my keys and car. Go, get out.

Dr. Beth: Thank you!

Trey: You're welcome. Just go!

She got up and went out the front door. Trey looked on from his desk. She got to the parking lot, pressing the unlock button while pointing it at different cars. She is looking to see which one lit up. She pressed it four times then hit her mark—an old black car with an old throwback dashboard. She got in the car, started the engine, put it in drive, and stepped on the gas as if she was home free. She punches on the gas doing about eighty on a straight road. Looking behind her, nothing is in sight. She gave the car a little more gas. Now she's doing about ninety miles per hour. She looked back again and saw nothing. She looked in the rearview mirror and, to her shock, she saw Jennifer looking back at her. She swung the car on the other side of the road, and back over again. Beth almost lost control of the car because she was scared. She hit the brakes. She pressed on them once, then twice. The car didn't stop.

Dr. Beth: Oh Shit!

Ch. 11

"Get Away"

She tapped the brakes again and again but the car won't stop. She looked down and saw the MPH. The car was going almost one-hundred twenty, maybe one-hundred thirty miles per hour, and she still can't stop it. In her sights, a beer truck is approaching fast with no intention of slowing down. If the truck comes across her, Dr. Beth will die. The beer truck is up to about seventy mph. It's going east to west. Dr. Beth is headed north to south at a high speed and cannot stop. Jennifer is controlling the gas. The truck driver blew his horn so she could slow down or stop. She's going too fast. The truck is too close to her for him to break it down. She has to be the one. She took both of her feet and pressed down on the brakes as hard as she can. The car will not stop or slow down. She got close, screaming and closing her eyes. She barely scraped the back of the truck as she nails biter bye. She got by. But by then the road that she was on is a dead end. So she whipped the car around really hard to the side. The car spun around and around like three or four times. Then it stopped, almost hitting the side rail. The car stopped. She turned towards the back seat where she saw Jennifer yell out.

Dr. Beth: What The Fuck Is Wrong With You?!!!! Tell me, what the hell do you want?

(The radio turned on) "I been really trying baby to hold on to you for so so long. If you feel the way I feel, then let's get it on".

She put the car back in drive and drove to her house. She pulled up to the driveway, sitting in the car, just looking at her house thinking to herself. That's my life. What I'm going through cannot be my life. All of the lights were off, except the porch lights, but that too turned off. All of a sudden, all of the lights in the house turned on, all at once.

Dr. Beth: Okay, Jennifer, what are trying to tell me?

She got out of the car rubbing her arms since it's a little bit chilly outside. She has low blood. She makes her way towards the house. She is wondering, "What's going on?" She got to the side door. She turns the doorknob right to left a few times trying to open the door. Dr. Beth stepped back and lifted the doormat to get the spare key. They always left it there just in case they lose their key. She put the key in and unlocked the door, pushing the door in before she took a step inside. The door makes a squeaky sound. She stopped and looked around, thinking to herself, "I have to go inside. If I don't go, then I won't know". She stepped inside, chancing it but being careful. She walked in and looked around. She walked through the den and picked up a short blanket to wrap herself in to stay warm. Then she ever so lightly took steps. She walked down the hallway, passing her mirror on the right and a coat closet on the left. She makes her way to another room. This is where it all started. Blood still on the floor. She's trying to remember what happened and why. She heard a voice that sounds like her husband saying, "Beth, please". She calls out to him, "Peter?" She is moving towards the steps looking at all of the dry blood everywhere. She starts to walk up the steps, one step, two, three, four, five, six, seven, eight, nine, and ten steps. She made it to the top and heard the voice again saying, "No, baby, no!!!" She is now looking over her left shoulder, remembering it all over again like it just happened an hour ago; seeing him in the hallway covered with blood and begging out to Beth, "Please, don't kill me". Looking down the hall from the bedroom, she stood there watching how it all happened: seeing herself in the same outfit from that night and coming out of the room with a large kitchen knife braced to her chest with Peter's blood all over it. She walks toward him. He yelled out, "Please, don't kill me. Please, Beth, what did I do? Why are you doing this to me?" She stood over him and put both hands on the handle of the knife. She raised her arms over her head and stabbed him ten times in the chest. She then whispered to him, "I'll always love you, Peter".

Beth saw how and what happened. She yelled, "NO!" Then tears start to roll down her face. It's blood all over the floor and walls where she killed Peter. She walked closer and closer to the spot. Then she looked on her wall and saw writing in blood saying, "I'M HERE WITH

YOU!" Dr. Beth just stared at it thinking to herself that she saw those words in the pictures that Sheriff Thomas had when he came to see her. Beth rubbed her face with her hands. She closed her eyes like she can't believe she did this to Peter. She walked back to their bedroom. She's looking around trying to pull herself together. She heard something in the bathroom. She starts to walk that way. She went into the bathroom seeing herself in the shower. She's washing away the signs of blood from killing Peter. Then she stepped out of the shower, drying her hair like nothing happened. She went over to the mirror and looked at herself face to face. As she was staring at herself, blood started to pour out of her nose. She screamed as she flicks her head side to side. She saw reflections of herself and Jennifer at the same time. Then Jennifer left her body. Beth just looked into the mirror trying to catch her breath. She felt her face and looked back into the mirror.

Ch. 12

"Remembering The Murder"

Dr. Beth: She wanted me to see that she killed Peter and used me to do it. Now I see.

She walked back to her bedroom and dropped to the floor and cried. Then she looked on their bedroom wall and saw a picture of her and Peter at a house on a piece of land that his parents left him. They use to go there sometimes. Around the front of it, it said, "I'M HERE WITH YOU". She cried. She is missing Peter. She thought about him sitting on the side of the bed with tears flowing down her face. She thought to herself, I miss you. The next morning, the sky was clear. It was a cool chill in the air. She got up holding the picture of her and Peter close to her heart. Beth took the blanket off. She slept in her clothes. She put on her shoes and headed out to the car to go to Peter's parent's house that they left him. By the time she got there, the sun was barely shining over the trees. The chill is still in the air. She parked the car, got out, and looked around. She is still wearing the same clothes that she had on last night. She has on a little jacket that she likes to wear and easily slip on. Beth walked up to the house. She took her first step to the house thinking, "Wow, it's been a long time". Beth walked up four steps and stood there. Then she got to the top of the porch. She looked left, then she looked right. She walked toward the right side of the house coming up on a window. Beth looked in. She got closer to get a better view of what's inside. She saw an old wooden table that's close to four chairs. In the far corner, a wooden chest with a knob missing and a few scratches on it by a windowpane. Beth saw that there is really nothing in there. She looked left and started walking in that direction. She walked past the front door, making her way to the end of the house, and looking at an outhouse on the side of the main one. It's patches of grass around the front yard. The wood is chipped up on the outhouse. It looks so old that the paint is starting to fall off on the ground. Beth walked over to the side door. She pushed it open and looked inside. It's dark inside so she can't really see much. She stepped inside to look around. All she saw were some dusty old things. She heard a sound and she starts to walk toward it. She's getting closer and closer by each step. When she looked, it jumped past her. Beth jumped back and screamed.

Dr. Beth: Wow, a cat? Damn, it was a cat.

She started to look around more after she caught her breath. She's looking and walking back from where she came in. She saw a passageway that was on the side of the inside of the outhouse when she first walked in. Beth didn't see it the first time. The outhouse looked like another small house, rich (which you can say the Dickson's were). Beth hit the latch on the double doors. They opened up like French doors, making a squeaky sound. Her mind is wandering back and forth. She is getting the feeling that something isn't right. She looks like she's getting scared. She took a look inside while standing at the edge of the doors. She's looking at the room up and down, but nothing is really there but some cans of paint on the table and a few boxes on the floor. Tools were hanging up against the wall all around the room. There is a short ladder in the corner. Just a lot of handyman things that have a lot of dust on it. Then something caught her eye as she stepped back out of the door and was about to close it. She saw a box that's halfway opened on a DVD's table. It looks like it's kind of new. She looked at it, then looked back around the room. She spotted a piece of the wall cracked with light coming through. Beth walked toward the door, moving things out of the way so she can get to the real reason for what was behind the door and why she's there. As she opened the door, dust and dirt fell. She waved her hand and arm back and forth to get the dust out of her face and coughing at the same time. She looked inside. It appeared to be a stairway to the basement. Beth is thinking about what could be down there. She looked behind her, then back at the stairs. Should she go or should she not, hmmm. She's going to take that chance. She's come too far now. She walked down the stairs looking. She got to the bottom and saw a white sheet hanging from one end to the other. Beth wants to know what's behind the sheet. Her head is turning back and forth like "what's this place". With every step, she's so careful. Beth put her hand on the sheet and stroked it across. She walked to see what was at the end of it. She takes her hand to pull the sheet back. She was shocked. What's really going on?

Ch. 13

"Secrets"

Dr. Beth: Where did this stuff come from? How did it get down here? On a small table, she spotted a laptop and a flat-screen TV, with DVDs right beside it. Across the laptop, with a camera on it, is a bed, a nightstand, and a box that has the words "put to good use" written on it. Beth wanted a clear look at everything down there. She found a light and turned it on. She saw a queen-sized bed, a table, a couch, a lamp, an icebox, books on the table, a laptop, a flat-screen TV, and so much more. She looked at the wall and saw a lot of rope, chains, and whips. On the floor is a box of needles and a medical bag inside it. She heard a noise behind her. The laptop screen lit up. She walked back toward it.

She pushed play and saw Peter cutting the neck and face off of a young girl. She hollered as he continued to record on the DVD. What Beth saw was heartbreaking. The DVD played on as she heard, "Goodbye, my child. See you in a few. You've been good". He got up and wiped the blood off of the knife with her panties. "Excellent", he said. Another masterpiece. Then he kissed her forehead. He walked over to the camera, looked into it, and smiled. "Do you like what you see?" A few seconds later, Dr. Beth heard footsteps up top. She looked up and saw a shadow of a person as the steps go by. She looked over by the medical bag and picked up the knife. She heard someone coming down the stairs. She's ready to meet whoever is coming. She got to the bottom of the stairs. The footsteps stopped. She looked up and no one was there. A hand touches her from behind. Dr. Beth jumped over to the stairs holding the knife up and said, "If you come near me, I'll cut you".

Officer: Put the knife down!

Dr. Beth: You drop the gun!

Officer: Please put the knife on the ground!

Dr. Beth: Drop that gun!

Officer: It's not gonna happen. Drop that knife!

Dr. Beth: Hell no, you drop it!

Officer: Holly shit, Dr. Beth, I know you.

Dr. Beth: What??

Then a girl grabbed Dr. Beth from behind and she was covered in blood. Dr. Beth screams. She broke loose and put her back up against the officer that was pointing the gun at her.

The girl: Please, please, you have to help me!

Officer: Who? What the fuck is going on? And who are you?

The girl had cuts going across her face. Cuts inside of her bra and panties with blood all over her body.

The girl: Please help!!

Officer: Willie, get down here now!!!

The girl: Help me please, please don't go!

An hour later, back at the sheriff's station, the sheriff was speaking to the news anchor outside of the building. He's giving a statement as the news of what has happened is sweeping all over the states.

Sheriff Thomas: All I can really tell you at this point is that the girl discovered this morning is known as Crystal Jones. She was reported missing a few weeks back. She was found alive by my officers at an estate that belongs to Dr. Peter Dickson. Ms. Jones is being seen and hospitalized at this time.

Reporter 1: Can she talk? Do you know that yet?

Reporter 2: Did she mention how she got there?

Sheriff Thomas: We can't speak on that as of this moment.

Reporter 3: Are there others?

Sheriff Thomas: I can't confirm that. Please excuse me.

Reporter 4: Sheriff, sheriff, we heard that the FBI is going to take over this case and investigate, true or false?

Sheriff Thomas: Hey! Why don't you ask the fucking FBI?

Sheriff Thomas turned and walked back into the building and ran into Dr. James.

Dr. James: Sheriff, we need Dr. Beth at the hospital for medication.

Sheriff Thomas: Are you out of your got damn mind?

Attorney: Consider house arrest pending trial, given the circumstances.

Sheriff Thomas: News, I'll give you news. Your client knocked out a guard last night, assaulted a nurse, and fucking escaped from an institution. Don't forget that her ass stole a car too.

Dr. James: Plus saved a girl's life.

Sheriff Thomas: How did she know she was there?

Dr. James: I can't tell you in a million years.

Attorney: We have no idea. But the point is...

Sheriff Thomas: The point is that the lady is still a murder suspect. Come here, attorney, I want to talk to you in private.

They met up face to face.

Sheriff Thomas: The FBI said there could be more victims. Look, there were needles in a medical bag. Also a laptop, with a camera down there. Once the press gets wind of this, it's going to get ugly. I need some answers. You know her, and I'm running out of time.

Dr. Allie Mae made her way to the room. They were holding Dr. Beth in at the sheriff's office with a guard. The door opened and Allie walked in. Beth is sitting in a chair with her hands on a five-foot tassel as the guard watches her.

Ch. 14

"Seeing The Same"

Allie Mae: Hi, I really need to speak with Dr. Beth, if you don't mind?

The guard replied, "Sure". He walked to a window and looked out while Dr. Allie Mae and Dr. Beth sat down and chat a bit.

Allie Mae: I've been racking my brain just to believe that Peter did this. Shocked, cold, and unheard of. We have put in a lot of years working together. I thought I knew your husband very well. I was way off.

Dr. Beth: Well, Allie, take it from me. You weren't the only one if I do say so myself.

Allie Mae: Do you believe my baby girl could have been one of Peter's victims?

Dr. Beth: I do believe that strongly.

Allie Mae: Hmmmm.

Dr. Beth: That's "WHAT I'M HERE WITH YOU" meant. Jennifer was trying to show me in so many ways that Peter was behind this and there are more.

Allie Mae: As time went by, we thought our Jen Jen committed suicide for whatever reason. You see, Dr. Beth, even after time and time has passed by...well.

Allie bit her lips and crossed her hands. Beth took her hand and put it on Allie's hand without saying anything. Then she said, "It's okay, tell me".

Dr. Beth: Tell me what's on your heart.

Allie Mae: I had this same thought over and over about my Jennifer. It became so strong that I started to take medication to clear it out.

Dr. Beth: Thoughts? What kind of Thoughts?

Allie Mae: My Jen Jen was in ghost form and in terrible pain. I couldn't help her.

Dr. Beth: I saw her the same way, in ghost form. What does that mean, Allie Mae?

Allie Mae: Beth, I …I….I didn't look for explanations. It's a thought, a deep thought, a delusion.

Dr. Beth: A deep thought of delusions that we both share.

They stare at each other. Then Allie started to think about Jennifer and began to cry a little. Then she told Dr. Beth she's going to go lay down for a while.

Allie Mae: You take care of yourself.

Dr. Beth: Family, right, you'd do the same.

Hours are passing. Dr. James was on his way to the office. His phone rings.

Dr. James: Hello!

Dr. Beth: James! I was just speaking with Allie Mae. I've been a little wrong about everything until now you see. The image is really crystal clear. The man who's been touching the women at the facility is somewhat connected to this as well. And it all goes back to that night. I saw it at Amanda's cell.

Dr. James: Beth, come on, don't do this, please. Am I getting through to you? Every time I start to take you seriously you go off the deep end again. Talking delusions this and delusions that. Let it go.

Dr. Beth: I'm not delusional, you ass! I'm possessed, know the difference!

Dr. James: Sorry to hear that. But me personally I don't believe in ghosts, Beth.

Dr. Beth: I don't either. But the bottom line is they believe in me. Me, James, me.

Dr. James: Really? Okay, really?

Dr. James hung up the phone and took a deep breath and rubbed his head. He's thinking to himself, "Why is this happening to me?"

Beth was still holding the phone up to her ear.

Dr. Beth: Fucker!!

Then she hung up the phone. The guard walked up behind her and grabbed her by the arm and said…

Guard: Let's go, please.

He took her back to her cell where she will wait.

Dr. Beth: Hey, listen, I really need to speak with Sheriff Thomas.

Guard: Step back, ma'am, while I close the cell door. He'll be back tomorrow; he's working with the FBI.

Dr. Beth: It's really, really important that I speak to him

Guard: Really? You're not going anywhere, lady.

Dr. Beth: I know that for now, but people's lives are on the line here.

Guard: I get that. But I have orders to watch you and keep you locked up.

Dr. Beth: Let's say I escape.

Guard: No way. I wasn't going to let you make a call, but I did just to be nice.

Dr. Beth: I know, a good deed. You seem like a good cop.

Guard: I am.

Dr. Beth: I get that.

Guard: Do you?

Dr. Beth: Yes.

Guard: Well, what you are thinking don't make me that much good, I can bet you that.

Dr. Beth: Here me out. If the real killer is still out there and I'm locked up in here, wouldn't that make you feel bad?

Guard: It's not my call.

Dr. Beth: Are you listening to me at all?

Guard: I heard everything you said.

Dr. Beth: Okay then, let me out.

Guard: Good speech won't work.

Dr. Beth: Asshole!

Guard: I tell you what, I'll leave the good sheriff a message.

Dr. Beth: Thank you.

Ch. 15

"Intersection"

The guard shut and locked the door. Dr. Beth watched him walk away. She went back and sat on the bed inside her cell. Meanwhile, Dr. James went back to his office, checking up on what Dr. Beth and him were talking about. He clicked his computer on. He goes to the internet and typed in the search box, "Ghosts' lonely souls". He sees all types of things pertaining to this. Religious, Mythological, Death, and Satanic. He sat back in his chair and began to think about everything he saw. Dr. Beth is still sitting in her cell bed. The lights start to blink on and off. She now knows that this is all too familiar. Then it stopped when she heard footsteps. The person coming down the hall is Sheriff Thomas, walking with a cup of coffee towards Beth's cell.

Sheriff Thomas: Dr. Beth, I got a message that you wanted to speak with me.

Dr. Beth: Yes!

Sheriff Thomas: Okay, here I am, doc.

Dr. Beth: I wanted to talk to you and maybe this time it will stick to your brain.

Dr. Beth stood up on both feet looking at the sheriff face to face, staring him down from the other side of the cell bars.

Dr. Beth: You know, last time we were face to face all you did was scream, pointing the finger and accusing me.

Sheriff Thomas: Hey! Is this what you really have for me?

Dr. Beth: Oh, no, no, no. I want to lay out the facts. Do you agree?

Sheriff Thomas: Do you have any idea what can happen to a sheriff once the FBI takes over?

Dr. Beth: No! What the hell has that got to do with facts, sheriff?

Sheriff Thomas: Tell me something, anything at all.

Dr. Beth: I'M HERE WITH YOU.

Sheriff Thomas: What was that?

Dr. Beth: HERE WITH YOU. I know what it means.

Sheriff Thomas: What?

Dr. Beth: There are two killers to this game.

Sheriff Thomas: Let me grab a chair and sit down for this.

Sheriff Thomas got him a chair and leaned it up against the wall on the outside of Dr. Beth's cell. Beth sat back on her bed while they talked about it.

Dr. Beth: Allie Mae and I both saw her daughter as a ghost calling for help. Then on top of that, I saw a sneak peek of Amanda being attacked by a man in her cell. You get it?

Sheriff Thomas: Not really!

Dr. Beth: I know it sounds crazy. And Dr. James doesn't believe me.

Sheriff Thomas: Wait, you told Dr. James?

Dr. Beth: Yes.

Sheriff Thomas: Really? When?

Dr. Beth: Later on today. Why?

Sheriff Thomas got up out of his chair. He reached into his pocket and got the keys out to unlock Dr. Beth's door. He opened it up, slid the door back, and walked inside looking at Dr. Beth and still drinking his coffee.

Sheriff Thomas: Well, I kind of believe you. And I don't know why he would dismiss it. So you actually saw a man in the cell with Amanda?

Dr. Beth: Yes, I saw him.

Sheriff Thomas: Well, I've heard of serial killers who run together like wolves and shit.

Dr. Beth: Yeah, it's an efficiency, mental, and discipline syndrome.

Sheriff Thomas: So we're looking for the disciplined?

Dr. Beth: Yes.

Sheriff Thomas: Who is it?

Dr. Beth: I don't know.

Sheriff Thomas: Oh, come on, you're a psychiatrist. Dig deep, Beth. Break it down.

Dr. Beth: Okay, he would have to be someone who grew up in a household, that came up from a broken home with one parent. Ninety percent of the time, the father isn't there.

Sheriff Thomas: I see, carry on.

Dr. Beth: He developed an obsessive, over-dependent relationship with his mother.

Sheriff Thomas: Obsessive?

Dr. Beth: Yes! As time passes by, it turned into some inappropriate sexual attraction. He probably even got off by torturing little kids or something. That's who he is to me.

The sheriff got a little closer to Beth on the bed thinking about all she just said.

Sheriff Thomas: Wow, that's fucked up. You know a guy like that? You know a guy that can just blend in with anybody?

Dr. Beth: Yes, oh, yes, they usually do.

Sheriff Thomas: Look, Beth, I'm not trying to scare you or anything like that. But if you're right, there may be another killer lose. He may be frantically trying to cover his own ass, and you are a big threat to this guy. Who knows how much more stuff you know?

Dr. Beth: I don't know anything like that.

Sheriff Thomas: You saw the man in the cell with Amanda. You found a girl who should have been dead at the same house that you and Peter owned.

Dr. Beth: Yeah, but I lucked up on her by instinct.

Sheriff Thomas: This guy will never see the inside of a courtroom. He has to cover his ass. He has to believe that Peter confessed to you what he was doing.

Dr. Beth: I understand that, but Peter never told, he never confessed to me.

Sheriff Thomas: Maybe he didn't spill it out all at once. Well, we're sitting here you and me. You know you're the psychiatrist. There's a lot of ways to confess. I'm just trying to connect the dots, put myself in those shoes for a better look.

She just stared at him.

Dr. Beth: Then why didn't he go back to his parent's house?

Sheriff Thomas: You mean take care and let the girl do away with the evidence?

Dr. Beth: That's correct.

Sheriff Thomas: Well, that's a panacy person. That's how you get caught. I think it's better to let things calm down. And then there's you. He's desperate.

Dr. Beth: Really? Desperate enough to open up to me?

Sheriff Thomas: Well, Beth, you're eighty percent correct. I kind of fit that profile. Long time friend of Peter. Best friend plus access to the facility. I never did get a kick out of hurting any kids, doc.

He looked at Dr. Beth with a mean face. She tries to make a break for it. He grabbed her by the hair. Yanked her back on the wall and tried to choke her. They struggle back and forth.

Dr. Beth: It was your sick twisted ass the whole time playing that role?

Sheriff Thomas: You were getting too close, nosey doctor.

The sheriff threw Dr. Beth up against the wall. He put his arm on the back of her neck, holding her in place as he pulled out his switchblade.

Dr. Beth: You can't kill me, sheriff!

Sheriff Thomas: Oh, no, I'd never do that. After I cut you every which way, I'm going to have a lot more fun with you than my best friend, Peter, ever dreamed.

Dr. Beth: Help, help!

The lights blinked off and on like it had a shortage in it. He turned and looked behind him. Then she bit him on the arm, put the knife up to the side of his neck, and cut him. He then took off running. He pulled his gun pointing it at Beth, took a shot, and missed. He went after her, yelling, "Beth!" He saw her on the other end of the hall by the ambulance gas pump. He took another shot. He missed her again. It hit the gas pipe enough to have gas shooting out of the side, making it hard for him to get past it. Beth went upstairs and banged on the glass door, yelling, "Somebody help me!" But it's after hours and everyone is gone for the day. Sheriff Thomas starts to walk up the stairs. Loosening his shirt, he took off as a cover so he can get past. He got to the top and Beth is still yelling. Then she ran out of that room to another, trying to get away. Thomas saw her and tried to grab her but he missed. She keeps on running and he goes after her. He's on Beth's heels. Right before he grabbed her by the hair, she sidesteps a chair and ran past it while the sheriff wasn't looking. He then flips right over it straight to the floor, giving Beth enough time to hide. He got up then yelled out, "You little fucker!!" He stood up and walked into the room, rubbing his hands together.

Sheriff Thomas: Well, well, well, I see you want to play a little cat and mouse.

He went into his back pocket and pulled out his work keys. Then he walked over to his glass case with all of his guns in it (a hobby of his is he loves guns).

Sheriff Thomas: You know what this is going to look like, Beth? You tried to escape. That gives me the right to stop you by any means necessary.

He reached in and got a highly powerful rifle, cocked it back, and started the cat and mouse hunt.

Sheriff Thomas: Jennifer wasn't the first on the list. Your dear husband, my best friend, Peter. Oh, yeah, Pete killed a girl when we were just pee-wees. I helped him bury the body and some.

He kicked the door open and let off a round, but no one was there.

Sheriff Thomas: Now that's what you call best friends forever.

He turned and pointed the gun at the TV. and put a hole right through it so strong that it didn't set off the desk or the floor.

Sheriff Thomas: We start getting older and older. Listen, we never lose our fuel for the young sweet girls.

Beth looked and saw a gun strapped under a desk. Clip already in there safely. All it needs now is just a free hand to get it safely off, Aim, and shoot.

Sheriff Thomas: You know we took a break for a few years. But my pal saw beautiful Jennifer and hell, let me tell you, that was a temptation wayyyy too deep not to try. Let me give you the inside. Me and Pete and those girls, we had the time of our lives, out at Peter's parent's house, away from everyone. Shit was perfect. What more could you ask for? Those were our little bitches. They would do any and everything we want them to do. We were the only things that mattered to them, but you...

He saw a shadow out of the corner of his eye and he turned. He put a hole in that door.

Sheriff Thomas: DR. BETH!!!!

He walked around laughing, trying to catch this little mouse.

Sheriff Thomas: Now, hey, good doc. You and I both know the only way you leaving is when they come and carry you out of here with a hole inside and out of you. So let's be clear and end this cat and mouse shit.

He looked up into the other room and saw a girl who looked like Dr. Beth standing there ready to fire. Her face looked like Beths', then changes to Jennifer, then back to every few seconds.

Sheriff Thomas: Yes, thank you. Dr. Beth, you know I always liked you.

He pointed the rifle at whoever it is through the glass into the other room and took a shot, breaking the glass. She's still standing there looking back at him as the offices are filling up with gas from the pipe. He stood there trying to clear his eyes, thinking, "Why is she still standing and looking back at him?"

Sheriff Thomas: DR. BETH?

But what Sheriff Thomas didn't realize was that Beth was looking at him from behind.

Sheriff Thomas: This isn't clear.

The sheriff starts to walk near her. He cocked the gun back and took another shot at her. When he got up, he realized that's not Beth, so he turns around and saw Beth standing there.

Sheriff Thomas: This isn't clear!!

Dr. Beth pointed the handgun at Sheriff Thomas and pulled the trigger, hitting him in the head. He falls to the floor with his mouth wide open. He drops dead. Dr. Beth stood there and watched him fall by her hands.

Dr. Beth: CLEAR IS OVERRATED TO MOST.

She walked out of the room, then into the room where she shot the sheriff. Beth walked over him as she held onto the gun, heading toward the front door that's made out of glass. Dr. James banged on the glass, making a thumping sound. She turned quickly to see what the noise is. She saw Dr. James look back at her, moving his lips.

Dr. James: I'm really sorry, Dr. Beth.

She dropped her and looked back at him, taking a deep breath like, "Now you see I'm not crazy". Hours later, after they got everything settled, she got her license reinstated as she quickly got back to work.

A week after that, late at night, Dr. Beth and her ex-patient, Amanda, are walking next to each other. They just left a diner for a late dinner. They started to walk and talk a little before saying their goodbyes.

Amanda: Wow, it's been a week and I still have ups and downs inside my mind. You know, doc, sometimes I wake up in fear and scream.

Dr. Beth: That's okay, Amanda, you're having a breakthrough.

Amanda: I understand, but this is like a bad dream, not good. You know, Dr. Beth, a lot of people thought you and I were crazy, but we showed them, more than they ever knew. I think once you make your bed, you have to lay in it.

Dr. Beth: No, no, Amanda, not so. I made a difference. I laid in it, then got up. Sad but it's true, hard but it's fare.

Amanda: I really hope that's true for you, Dr. Beth. My plane leaves in half an hour.

Dr. Beth: Oh, I hate to see you go. But okay I'll get you a cab so you can be on time.

Dr. Beth held out her hand to flag down a cab so Amanda could be on her way to the airport.

Dr. Beth: I really love the dress you have on, it's very pretty.

Amanda: Thank you, doctor. I love your shoes, they're so hot.

They both laughed and started to hug each other as they say their goodbyes, maybe forever.

Dr. Beth: Well, good luck with your new beginning and your job. Okay?

Amanda: I, I wanted to really thank you from the bottom of my heart for everything you have done. You, you really helped me, Dr. Beth.

Dr. Beth: I helped you but you also helped me. You taught me how to listen.

Amanda: I'll never forget you. Thank you.

Dr. Beth: I'll never forget you. Make us proud. We beat all odds, you and I share a bond.

They hugged one last time that night. Amanda started to cry. Seems Dr. Beth was already shedding tears. They smile at one another and held hands, then let go as Dr. Beth watches Amanda get back into her cab for her new beginning. Dr. Beth waved goodbye and smiled. Amanda smiled and waved. As the cab drove away with Amanda, Dr. Beth started to walk off on the sidewalk feeling good. She had a new haircut, nice and short, as she too has a new beginning to look forward to. She smiles and thinks to herself. The wind is blowing in her face ever so lightly. She walks, then looks, and stopped at the edge of the sidewalk. She saw a little girl by herself across the street looking back at her. A city bus is coming on her side as the little girl stepped out in front of it seconds away from being hit. The bus is not slowing down. The little girl reaches out for Dr. Beth. Beth has this blank look on her face trying to speak but she can't. Just before the bus got close to the little girl and made an impact, Dr. Beth reached and yelled, "No!!!"

And the bus went through the little girl as it passed by. All she saw was a bus passing and no little girl. It was like her mind was playing tricks on her, but seeing that just happen means something. It's always something. She gasps for air. As she was walking up the road, she saw a flyer on a pole with that missing little girl's face on it, the girl she just saw seconds ago. The flyer reads: HAVE YOU SEEN, KIM? MISSING CHILD.

THE END

Written by Bobby Boyd